OTTER CHAOS!

Other Awesome Animal titles available:

Coming Soon:

OTTER CHAOS!

MICHAEL BROAD

Illustrated by Jim Field

HarperCollins *Children's Books*

First published in Great Britain by HarperCollins *Children's Books* 2013
HarperCollins *Children's Books* is a division of HarperCollins*Publishers* Ltd,
77-85 Fulham Palace Road, Hammersmith, London W6 8JB

www.harpercollins.co.uk

1

Text copyright © Michael Broad 2013
Illustrations copyright © Jim Field 2013

Michael Broad and Jim Field assert the moral right to be identified as the
author and illustrator of this work.

ISBN 978-0-00-748973-2

Printed and bound in England by
Clays Ltd, St Ives plc

To my big sister, Jackie.
For our adventures along the river.

In the Black corner...

In the Brown corner...

Chapter One

The Family Meeting

After a long, lazy day of chasing fish and skimming stones, Woody waved goodbye to Sooty, and the two otter pups headed for their homes on opposite banks of the river. The pair had only met a few weeks earlier, but were already the best of friends.

"See you tomorrow, Sooty!" yelled Woody Brown as his furry black friend reached the other side of the river and clambered on to the grassy bank.

"See you tomorrow, Woody!" Sooty Black yelled back, waving both arms at his furry brown friend. Then Sooty dashed along the water's edge and vanished into the roots of an overhanging tree that concealed his family den.

A tangle of twigs and branches marked the entrance to Woody Brown's riverside home. Woody dived below the waterline

with a tail splash, whooshed through the tunnel entrance and clambered up into a cavern lined with mud, twigs and moss.

The world above had been serene, with humming insects and busy buzzing bees, but down in the den there was a rollicking riot of otter activity!

"What's going on?" gasped Woody, trying not to get flattened as his entire family scampered out of three narrow tunnels and squeezed into the central chamber. But the only replies he got were an "OUCH!" and an "EEEK!" and an "OI! GET OFF MY HEAD!"

It seemed Papa Brown had summoned everyone for an emergency meeting. This meant three generations of the Brown family had to cram themselves into a very small space and no one had the faintest idea why. Papa did a quick headcount of nine, including his own, and then wriggled through the furry throng and lapped his paws for everyone to be quiet.

"Big families are brilliant!" he said cheerfully, which was met with a wave of groans and grumbles from the tangle of hot, squashed otters. "But I think we can all agree that, living in this tiny den together, things can get a little... er... heated...'

"Do get to the point, dear," said Mama Brown, fanning Grandma Maple and Grandpa Bruno with her tail. "Or soon there will be two fewer otters to hear your fabulous news."

"Yes, of course," said Papa, swiftly trimming a long-winded speech about big families in his head. "When I left the den this morning I thought today would be an ordinary day of fishing and floating and cracking clams on my furry belly. Little did I know that fate had other ideas..."

"An even shorter version than that, my love," sighed Mama.

"Yes, dear," said Papa, cutting his dramatic build-up down to the bare essentials. "I was swimming upstream, heading for my usual fishing spot, when I suddenly saw—"

"Oi! Get your tail off my tail!" snapped Nutmeg, prodding her twin brother in the chest.

"It's not my tail, it must be your tail!" snapped Chestnut, prodding his sister back.

"Actually, I think that's my tail," whispered Beanie, wiggling the end of it just to make sure. Beanie was younger than the twins and a little older than Woody. She preferred snacking to swimming and daydreaming to diving, which meant she still had most of her puppy fat.

"That's one enormous tail!" chuckled the twins.

"Oh, never mind roly-poly Beanie and her chubby club," scoffed Coco, frantically licking her paws and smoothing them over her head. "My fur is frizzing up in this humid hole!"

"Don't be so mean to Beanie," said Woody, standing up for his shy sister, even though Coco was the biggest and he was the smallest. "At least she isn't a frizzy-furred old stinky bottom!"

"HA! HA!" laughed Chestnut and Nutmeg.

"Ooo, you little...!" shrieked Coco, lunging for her little brother, which proved difficult to do in such a tight space, so she ended up on top of everyone.

The young otters all began squabbling, which they often did, having spent their whole lives sharing one small chamber between the five of them. And they were squabbling so ferociously they missed Papa's big news. He pressed his paws either side of his whiskers and yelled it again at the top of his voice.

"WE'RE MOVING HOME!" he boomed.

Grandma Maple and Grandpa Bruno snapped awake, while Woody, Beanie,

Nutmeg, Chestnut and Coco fell silent for a whole two seconds before they all leapt forward to ask the same question.

"Can I have my own room?" they pleaded. "PLEEEEEEASSSE!"

"Yes," smiled Papa Brown. "You may have your own chamber."

"Who?" asked Beanie and Woody, wondering which of their siblings they would no longer have to share with. "Who's getting their own room?"

"I should get it!" said Chestnut. "Nutmeg snores!"

"I should get it!" said Nutmeg. "Chestnut farts!"

"I should get it!" demanded Coco. "I'm

the eldest and by far the prettiest!"

"Actually, all five of you will have your own chambers," Papa smiled proudly. "And there will be one for me and Mama, and another for Grandma and Grandpa, and one left over!"

Now he had his family's undivided attention, Papa Brown told everyone about the enormous den he'd found abandoned upstream, waving his paws about as he described the grand scale and sprawling layout of their brand-new home. It was called Cottonwood Lodge and was a mud-caked mansion compared to the cramped conditions they currently lived in. They would be swapping three small chambers

with three narrow connecting tunnels for eight large chambers with a network of six wide tunnels, and an indoor splash pool, and mooring pad, and a mudslide and storage galore!

"Who used to live there?" asked Mama

Brown, eyes glazing over as she began mentally decorating with sludge, twigs and the finest moss, while allocating chambers and stores for their supplies.

"I found out from a passing river rat that the lodge belonged to a beaver and his wife and their ten little kits," said Papa. The otters gathered round, bright eyes sparkling as they imagined their new home. "He built extension after extension as his family grew, but eventually there were just too many children to fit, so they had to move on."

"That was one busy beaver!" said Mama Brown.

"When are we going?" asked Coco. She was keen to have her own room where she could tend to her appearance all day long, away from annoying brothers and sisters who rubbed her fur up the wrong way.

"With prime property like that we don't want anyone else moving in, so there's no time to lose," said Papa. "We will head off first thing in the morning, which means you should all get an early night."

There was a snuffle from the corner of the chamber where Grandpa Bruno and Grandma Maple had already made a head start, having fallen asleep in a cosy cuddle.

"There's a lot of packing to do," said Mama. "So we'll be relying on you all to be responsible for your own bedding and anything else you want to take with us."

"Yes, Mama!" the otters said excitedly and dashed off to gather their few belongings before their last night of sharing a chamber. And for the first time ever there were no arguments between the brothers and sisters because they were too excited about the new home. They were all lost in their own thoughts about what their new chambers would be like.

Coco imagined sitting in her room, smoothing her fur dreamily.

Chestnut imagined a room with no Nutmeg and no snoring.

Nutmeg imagined a room with no Chestnut and no farting.

And Beanie imagined daydreaming all day and having midnight feasts on her own.

Woody simply looked forward to having his own space, a place without warring twins or a vain big sister who was always in a mood. Beanie was no trouble at all, but it would be nice to have a room where he could have other pups over to play. He couldn't wait to tell his best friend—

"Sooty!" gasped Woody, suddenly realising that moving upstream to another section of the river would mean leaving his friend behind. It was hard enough meeting up now with their dens on opposite banks of the river, but the extra distance would make it impossible for the young pups to see each other.

Woody leapt out of bed and hurried to his parents' chamber, which was empty, so he swam out of the den and up to the surface to find the riverbank full of thin branches and reeds. Mama and Papa were busy building rafts by moonlight.

"I don't want to move upriver!" he said. "I want to stay here."

"Why would you want to stay in this tiny den when you can live at Cottonwood Lodge?" asked Papa, bending the thin branches and tying them with riverweed. "Don't you want to have your own room any more?"

"I do," sighed Woody, sitting down heavily on the bank. "It's just that Sooty lives on the other side of the river and I don't want to leave him behind."

"Oh, I'm sure he will understand," said Mama, setting her weaving aside to stroke Woody's head. "And when we're all settled

 26

you can invite him to come and stay with us. There will be plenty of room in the new place and you can show him around the neighbourhood."

"Can Sooty really come and stay?" asked Woody, feeling excited again.

"Of course," said Papa. "The more the merrier!"

"Now hurry off to bed," said Mama. "We're all going on a very big adventure tomorrow, but moving home is hard work so everyone needs a good night's sleep."

"Yes, Mama!" said Woody.

The young pup dived into the river with a splash and scurried back to his chamber where his siblings were all sleeping soundly.

Woody was now more excited than ever about the move because he could explore a whole new section of river with his best friend and have sleepovers too. He could just imagine Sooty's face when he told him about the indoor splash pool and the mudslide at Cottonwood Lodge. What fun they were going to have together!

Chapter Two

A Whole New World

At the first light of dawn, the Brown family were already turfing out their beds and belongings, shoving them through the entrance of the den and letting everything float to the surface, to be piled on to the bobbing rafts. Mama and Papa had built a large one for the bedding and four smaller ones for supplies. The rafts were all anchored at the bank so everyone could add the last of their stuff.

"Can I take this rock?" panted Chestnut, heaving a small boulder above the waterline, legs paddling frantically as he fought to stay afloat.

"Like there won't be rocks where we're going," Nutmeg sighed sarcastically, tossing her collection of clamshells on the raft. "What's so special about that one?"

"It's my favourite rock for smashing shellfish," said Chestnut, cradling his rock like a baby and stroking it lovingly. "I really don't think I can live without it."

"You can take it if you carry it," said Papa.

"Never mind," shrugged Chestnut, and he hurled it over his shoulder.

The rock landed in a puddle on the bank and sent a great muddy SPLASH all over Coco, who had just come to the end of her lengthy morning grooming ritual.

"MY FUR!" she shrieked. "MY BEAUTIFUL, WATERPROOF FUR!" She dived into the water after Chestnut, who raced round in circles until his big sister got tired and gave up the chase.

"Can I ride on the big raft?" asked Beanie, packing the last of her snacks away with the food stores. She then took a handful back to cram in her mouth. "The one with all the bedding on it."

"That's for Grandma and Grandpa," said Papa. He lowered his voice to a whisper. "They're a bit too old to swim against the current and they keep falling asleep."

"There's nothing wrong with my hearing," said Grandpa Bruno, grey whiskers bristling indignantly. "And for your information I used to swim this river twice a day when I was your age."

"What are they saying?" asked Grandma Maple, lifting a horn-shaped hearing-shell up to her ear. There was nothing wrong with her hearing either, she just liked to pretend there was so she could eavesdrop more effectively.

"They think we're too old to swim against the current!" yelled Grandpa Bruno.

"We *are* too old to swim against the current!" Grandma yelled back, elbowing her husband in the ribs. "Now help me on to that nice big raft with all the comfy bedding. I feel like a nap."

"Twice a day I'd swim this river," Grandpa mumbled to himself as he hopped on to the raft piled high with grass and moss and hauled his wife up after him. "Back when I was in training…"

"I know you did," said Grandma, patting her husband's paw.

Further along the bank, Woody had finished packing his collection of amusingly shaped pebbles and was helping to load the last of the food stores, while keeping a constant vigil on the opposite bank. He was hoping to catch sight of Sooty before they left because there was no time to cross the river and tell him the news in person.

"I'm sure your friend will understand when you explain that we had to move fast before another family nabbed Cottonwood Lodge," said Mama, packing down the supplies and tying the rafts together. "And we can send word back by river rat as soon as we get there."

Woody knew his mama was right and decided to focus on the adventure ahead. The young pup had never moved house before – he'd never even been that far up the river – and he was sure Sooty wouldn't want him to miss out on all the fun.

"The current is picking up," yelled Papa, standing on a log with his tail dangling in the water. By wiggling his bottom, he was able to test the exact tug and flow of the river. "It's now or never, otters!"

Papa dived into the water and pulled up the rock anchors of the rafts so they began to drift out across the river, while Mama swam up and down, organising the moving party. Grandma Maple and Grandpa Bruno were perched on the bedding on the central raft and everyone else was in the water, positioned at different points along the train of smaller rafts.

"Goodbye, old home," said Beanie. "We

will miss you."

"I won't miss sharing a room with you lot!" scoffed Coco.

"And I won't miss snoring sisters!" said Chestnut.

"I definitely won't miss farting brothers!" said Nutmeg.

"New home, here we come!" yelled Woody.

"HOORAY!" cheered the Browns as they began their journey, all swimming together and pushing the chain of reedy rafts up the river as they headed for a whole new world.

That whole new world and their new home were only some hundred metres upriver. In fact, they could have seen

Cottonwood Lodge from their old home if they had stood on a rock and looked in that general direction. Still, it was a huge adventure for the family and everyone was very excited.

Things got even more exciting just a few moments later when the river quickened, the rafts broke their tethers and each of them floated away in a different direction, spinning and bobbing like rubber ducks in a whirlpool.

"HOLD ON TO THE NEAREST RAFT!" yelled Papa, who was gripping the bedding raft with Grandma and Grandpa. He was swimming with all his might to keep it moving upstream and not get carried off by the current.

The smaller store rafts that had spread out were now divided between the Browns. Mama had one, the twins had another and Beanie and Woody shared the third, leaving Coco one all to herself. The otters were swimming hard to push the rafts upstream. All except Coco, who perched on top of hers, busily flattening down her fringe, completely unaware that she was drifting away from her family on the ever-increasing rapids.

"COCO!" yelled Mama. "GET OFF THAT RAFT!"

"I don't want to get wet," the otter sighed wearily, and only then looked up to see that

she had left the convoy and was floating quickly downstream. Coco perched on the edge of the raft and gazed fearfully into the rushing water.

"JUMP!" cried Mama. "Don't worry about the supplies!"

"I'm not," huffed Coco. "But I've just dried my fur!"

41

"JUMP IN RIGHT NOW, YOUNG LADY!" Mama shouted sternly.

Coco rolled her eyes and dived into the water, paws paddling frantically, so it took her no time to catch up with the otter flotilla.

"Is everyone still with us?" asked Papa. He climbed on to the bedding raft, looking out to count heads along the three remaining smaller vessels. Mama and the five young otters were all present and accounted for, and all they had lost was one raft of food.

"HOORAY!" cheered the Browns, who like most otters were generally optimistic and preferred to look on the bright side.

42

Only Beanie still looked fretful and raised a paw to get Papa's attention.

"It's OK, Beanie," Papa said kindly. "We won't run out of food."

"I wasn't thinking about the food," she frowned, even though she had been thinking about the lost supply raft moments earlier. "I was just wondering where Grandma had gone."

Everyone looked up at the top of the bedding raft to see Grandpa Bruno fast asleep on his back, who just then snuffled awake and said, "Are we there yet?" Then he stared, wide-eyed, at the empty space beside him.

"Nobody panic; she can't have gone

very far," said Papa, scratching his head and looking up and down the river. "Now, I don't think she could have fallen off the raft…"

"I didn't hear a splash," said Mama.

"And there are no giant eagles in these parts that might have carried her away," said Papa, looking at the sky and scratching his chin. "Not that I know of, anyway."

"Everyone be quiet," said Grandpa Bruno. "I hear snoring."

"Are you sure it's not Nutmeg?" said Chestnut.

"Shut up, farty bottom!" said Nutmeg.

"SHHHH!" hissed everyone else.

The Brown family held their breath as

Grandpa Bruno crouched down and pressed his head against the tall heap of bedding. Then he started digging in the wet grass and moss and hauled Grandma Maple back up to the surface, where she continued to snore, not realising that she'd been lost and found again.

"Well, I think we've had our quota of bad luck, with runaway rafts and vanishing grannies!" chuckled Papa, standing up on the raft as the streamlined flotilla continued along the river. "So I have every reason to believe it will be plain sailing from now on."

"HOORAY!" cheered the Browns for the third time that day.

Unfortunately, just as Papa was giving his speech, the raft passed under a low-hanging tree branch. The branch itself was high enough to clear easily, but the bees' nest dangling from it collided with Papa's head and joined the otters in their removals upstream. Unlike the otters, the bees rather liked where they were living, and were none too happy to get bashed off their branch on to a heap of wet grass that smelled like fish and elderly otters.

"BZZZZZ!" the bees buzzed angrily, pouring out of the nest. Then they gathered into a swarm and zoomed furiously towards the otters, who all squeaked in alarm and dived deep underwater before fleeing upstream.

With the rafts otter-free, the bees flew back to their branch and set about building a new nest, and without otters to propel them forward, the rafts quietly drifted back downstream too.

When the Browns finally arrived at their new home, they were a lot lighter than when they left, having first lost a raft of food, lost and found Grandma Maple and then lost everything else in a cloud of angry bees. But as they hauled themselves on to the sprawling island of twigs and branches that was Cottonwood Lodge, the family knew it had all been worth it.

"Now, don't worry about our stuff," panted Papa, standing at the entrance to the den and looking rather bedraggled. "We will find new bedding and build up our stores again in no time."

"The important thing is that we made it here in one piece," added Mama, staggering up to join her husband and wringing out her tail. "Now let's catch our breath before we explore our new home!"

"HOORAY!" cheered the Browns, and they collapsed in a heap.

Moments later the otter family bustled through the main tunnel of the den in much the same way as they always did, with squeals of "OUCH!" and "EEEK!"

and "OI! GET OFF MY HEAD!" But once they had all squeezed through the entrance, Cottonwood Lodge opened up into a spacious reception chamber, with a freshwater pool and mounds of moss for lounging around on. The chamber was lit through gaps in the twigs above and led off into many other tunnels, into which the Browns scampered excitedly to explore.

"Look at the size of these bed chambers!" gasped Mama, dashing with Papa from one room to the next, patting the mud-caked walls as if she couldn't believe her eyes. "The pups really can have one each!"

"I take it we'll be getting rid of the beaver droppings?" said Grandma Maple, poking her head in after them and frowning at the mess on the floor.

"And there's a whiff of wee that's making my eyes water," said Grandpa Bruno, flapping a paw in front of his nose. "Though it doesn't smell like any beaver I've ever encountered."

"It does need a good clean, but I think it's wonderful!" said Mama, kissing Papa on the nose and giving him a cuddle. And because the grandparents were also secretly thrilled despite their gripes and grumbles, they did the same.

The four of them made their way back to the central chamber just as the pups returned from their own explorations. The little ones were wide-eyed and breathless, exhilarated by what they'd discovered.

"There's a mooring pad and a log slide at the back!" yelled Woody, jumping up and down with excitement.

"And there are stepping stones leading all the way to the bank," gasped Coco. "So we don't always have to swim outside and get our fur wet needlessly!"

"There's loads of storage for food!" said Beanie, grinning broadly.

"And we've chosen our rooms!" cried Nutmeg and Chestnut, who ran out of two different tunnels and started dancing together, holding paws. "And they're so far apart we won't be able to hear or smell each other at all!"

"So you all like your new home?" asked Mama and Papa.

"WE LOVE IT!" cheered the otters, and they all joined in with Nutmeg and Chestnut, holding each other's paws and

dancing round the pool. Mama danced with Papa, Grandma Maple danced with Grandpa Bruno, Woody danced with Beanie, while Coco danced by herself, flicking her fur dreamily and trying to keep it completely dry.

The Browns were so busy dancing and laughing and being happy with their brand-new den, that no one noticed a large dark figure stomping through the entrance tunnel, snorting indignantly at the sight of them.

"Oh, no, you don't!" it growled. "This is *my* den!"

Chapter Three

A Blast From the Past

The Brown family stopped dancing and abruptly froze like musical statues, and then all turned their heads to see a big black otter looming in the entrance to the lodge. He looked very cross, snorting through his bristly black nostrils.

"Did you hear me?" he growled. "This is *my* den!"

"I'm sorry, but I think you've made a mistake," said Papa, stepping out in front of his family to settle what was obviously just a big misunderstanding. "I found this den yesterday and staked my claim by scratching here and here," he said, pointing at carved marks in a tree branch and neat little scrapes in the mud walls. "And if you take a sniff you'll detect a dot of musk and wee-wee over by the entrance there."

The black otter sniffed and raised an unimpressed eyebrow.

"Well, I found it yesterday too and drenched the whole place from top to bottom with my own musk and wee-wee, scenting every nook and cranny so everyone knows it's mine," he said, advancing into the chamber and rising tall on his hind legs. "Go on, take a whiff! It's pungent stuff and proves that I am the rightful owner."

The Browns all sniffed the unmistakable scent and screwed up their noses. What they had believed to be beaver wee or a rotting rodent, was indeed otter musk, albeit a particularly foul vintage.

"That horrid stink definitely wasn't here when I discovered the den yesterday," said Papa, rising up on his back legs too. "Which only proves that I got here first, and I have a whole family to look after."

"So do I," said the black otter, and he whistled through his claws.

Eight more black otters in various shapes and sizes immediately scurried down the tunnel and into the central chamber. Mama Black was first, looking very displeased at the sight of another family in her new reception and occasional spa room. She was followed by Grandpa Black and six pups, the youngest of which wriggled its way to the front of the family group.

The Browns and the Blacks faced each other across the freshwater pool. Neither was prepared to budge from their new home and all were wondering what would happen next and who would make the first move.

No one expected that it would be little Woody Brown, who pushed his way forward between Chestnut and Nutmeg and jumped in the middle of the pond, waving his paws excitedly.

"Sooty!" gasped Woody, splashing over to his best friend, who just happened to be the youngest pup in the family of black otters.

"Woody!" gasped Sooty, dashing forward and jumping in the pond too.

The rest of the otters, black and brown alike, watched with wide-eyed

bewilderment as the two young pups hugged and held paws and began bouncing up and down with glee. They were so excited to see each other they didn't even realise that everyone else was getting soaked.

"Enough!" growled a gruff and grizzly

voice from the back of the crowd as Grandpa Black came strutting forward. The old otter was big and burly with grey and white whiskers, though no less imposing for his age. "We are not leaving this den!"

"Neither are we!" growled a voice from the back of the Browns.

Grandpa Bruno barged to the front, all puffed up to match his black-furred opponent. The two otters circled the pond, sizing each other up. It was a curious dance, full of menace, that was nothing like the happy rejoicing of their grandsons, and both families were taken aback by the old otters' strange behaviour. Things got even stranger as the grandpas jumped into the pool, still facing each other, and began to skip from paw to paw, bobbing and weaving like deranged herons. As they got close, Grandpa Bruno suddenly froze, leant forward and squinted at the black otter's face.

"Big Bad Jack!" he growled, eyes flaring with recognition. "After all these years, you dare to show your big ugly face around these parts again."

"Well, if it isn't my old boxing partner, Bruno Brown," scoffed the black otter. "Knocking you out once obviously wasn't enough if you're coming back for more."

"You wouldn't have beaten me the first time if you'd fought fair," growled Grandpa Brown. "It should have been me that won the championship and you know it."

"Still crying foul, I see," snorted Grandpa Black.

"Still cheating honest folk out of what's rightfully theirs, I see," growled Bruno.

The two otters went nose to nose, snorting through their nostrils, grey whiskers bristling together.

"Enough!" yelled Grandma Maple, nudging forward and grasping Grandpa Bruno's paw. She tugged with all her strength until she managed to drag her fuming husband away from his black-furred rival. "I've lived through this silly rivalry once, and I'm not about to do it again," she mumbled, leading Grandpa Brown to the exit.

"Huh?" said everyone else.

Chapter Four

Destined for Stardom

"Grandpa was a boxer?" asked Woody Brown, scratching his head as his family followed the old otters outside to find them standing on the riverbank. They might as well have said Grandpa was a ballet dancer for all the sense it made because all he ever did was sleep and moan.

"Some things are best left in the past," said Grandma Maple, sitting on a log and fanning her face. The old otter seemed more troubled than her husband at the unexpected arrival. "Your grandpa doesn't like to talk about it, so we should respect his—"

"I was not just a boxer, young Woody," sighed Grandpa, sitting down next to his wife and holding her paw, his eyes glazing over as he recalled his glory days. "I was a super heavyweight champion, four years undefeated! 'Bruising Bruno Brown' they called me."

"And Big Bad Jack was your arch-enemy?" asked Woody.

"No," Grandpa said sadly as the mists of time descended and all of his memories came flooding back. "'*Jumping* Jack Black', as they called him back then, was my best friend in the whole wide world…"

After a long, lazy day of chasing fish and skimming stones, young Bruno Brown and Jack Black basked on the riverbank, talking excitedly about the start of the new boxing season. They were not only the very best of friends, having grown up together on opposite banks of the same river, they were also otter boxing champions in their own weight classes.

Bruising Bruno Brown was the reigning super heavyweight, and Jumping Jack Black was the reigning heavyweight, a class below his friend. They had climbed the ranks of the Otter Boxing Federation together from pups. They trained and sparred together along the riverbanks and supported each other in pursuit of their sporting dreams. The two young otters were destined for stardom.

"I can't wait to get back in the ring," said Bruno. "It has been a brilliant summer, but I'm itching to start competing again. If I manage to defend my title, I'll be the first otter to win the super heavyweight tournament five years in a row."

"You'll wipe the floor with all of them,"

laughed Jack. "There's not another otter along the whole river who's as fast on his paws as you. Except me, of course."

"True," laughed Bruno. "It's a good job we'll never have to fight each other. We're so well matched in speed and strength, I can't even guess who would win!"

"Well, luckily we'll never have to find out," said Jack, hurling another large fish in his mouth and rubbing his big, full belly. "What with us being in different weight classes and me being so much lighter," he added, and burped like a foghorn.

The two friends laughed loudly, happy in the knowledge that their boxing careers were on the up, and relieved that they would not be forced to compete against each other.

Yet, when it came to the vital weigh-in before the first bouts of the tournament, there was a huge surprise in store for both of them. Bruising Bruno weighed the same, but Jumping Jack Black tipped the scales out of the heavyweight class and into super heavyweight. His boxing name changed to Big Bad Jack and the new weight class meant that, if they both stayed long enough in the tournament, the friends would eventually have to fight each other.

Bruno and Jack made a pledge that day that whatever the outcome they would remain friends and would cheer each other on. But as they fought and kept winning their matches, Bruising Bruno and Big Bad Jack spent less and less time together. It was around then that Bruno met a beautiful young otter named Maple…

"Oh, let's not dredge up the past," said Grandma Maple, shooing the imaginary mists of time away with her flapping paws. "It's all so long ago, there's no need to open old wounds."

"Aw, tell us what happened, Grandpa!" begged the young otters. The Brown pups were all gathered round their grandparents, lying on their bellies, utterly engrossed in the story. Their parents were just as curious, since neither had any idea that the old otters had led such a thrilling life together.

"It was the last night of the tournament," said Grandpa, as the mists of time descended once again. "Jack and I had won all of our bouts over many weeks. We cleared the quarter-finals and semi-finals, and were warming up on opposite sides of the river before the final fight that would decide who would become the super heavyweight champion…"

72

"Promise me you'll be all right," said Maple, pacing up and down nervously while Bruno skipped and cross-skipped with a length of rope. "I don't know what I'd do if anything happened to you…"

"I'll be fine," Bruno said confidently. "I know Jack's moves better than he knows them himself. By the end of the night I'll be the first ever five-time super heavyweight champion."

"Then what?" sighed Maple, sitting on a log.

Bruno stopped skipping and frowned. He wasn't used to having anyone worry about him getting hurt. The otter tossed the rope away and held Maple's paws within his gloves.

"I'll be fine," he said again. "And when I win

this tournament, the Otter Boxing Federation will take me on a grand boxing tour up and down the river, and you can come with me. We'll be living the high life, Maple Moo!"

The crowd was becoming restless for the match to begin. Otters squeaked, river rats shrieked and beavers beat their tails. Bruno nuzzled with his lovely Maple and then headed for the ring where Big Bad Jack was already waiting, biding his time before—

"Your grandpa lost the match and that was the end of that," said Grandma Maple abruptly, breaking the spell of the story. "Now, is it lunchtime yet? I for one am feeling a bit peckish."

"Aw, Grandma!" groaned the young otters.

"Your grandmother is right," said Mama Brown. "We know that Grandpa didn't win the match, so he probably doesn't want to relive it all over again."

"*I didn't lose!*" said Grandpa Bruno, standing up and shaking a fist in the air. "I was robbed of my title by a scoundrel who pretended to be my friend. And I think our young Woody needs to know the truth about the otters he's mixing with. Now, where was I? Ah, yes. It was the final fight..."

Bruising Bruno Brown entered the ring and stepped up to his opponent. Before the river-rat referee could signal the start of the fight, Big Bad Jack reached out to shake his friend's paw. Bruno was only too pleased to put their friendship before everything else, just like they had promised in their pact, but when Jack let go, he wiped his glove over his head, slicking down his fur. Bruno had never seen his friend do this before, so he looked down at his own glove to see that it was glistening in the moonlight. A sniff confirmed that it was covered in fish oil, but before he could do or say anything, the referee rang the bell for Round One.

With oil on his right glove, Bruising Bruno couldn't throw a decent punch without it sliding off-target and Big Bad Jack's slicked-down fur made him untouchable. Bruno was a great fighter, but his failure to connect a single blow to his opponent meant it was only a matter of time before Jack beat him down.

And then Jack threw an uppercut that hit Bruno square on the jaw and lifted him off his feet. The brown otter sailed through the air as if in slow motion, and landed flat on his back with an enormous thud. The next thing he remembered was the knockout count from the ratty referee and Jack Black lifting his arms *in triumph, the crowd cheering and chanting his name.*

"And that was the last boxing tournament I ever competed in," sighed Grandpa Bruno. "Big Bad Jack became a sporting celebrity and went on tour with the Otter Boxing Federation, while I stayed at home to take care of your grandma, who I found out after the match was expecting pups in the spring."

The Brown family were quiet and thoughtful at the end of Grandpa's story. They didn't know what to say to the old otter who had lived such an amazing life.

"Where can I get some of that fish oil?"

asked Coco, who cared mostly about adding a really nice sheen and an additional layer of waterproofing to her grooming regime.

"From fish, of course," laughed Nutmeg and Chestnut.

"Oh, yes!" chuckled Coco.

"Why did you stop boxing, Grandpa?" asked Beanie, who was much more sensitive than her older siblings. "Could you not enter the next tournament and win back your title?"

"Oh, by the time next season started I had a young family and, without Jack to train with, I fell out of shape," he said, and then sat up and visibly brightened. "But now I have you lot and wouldn't change

79

that for all the titles in the world."

The Brown pups jumped up and gave their grandpa a big hug.

Woody felt bad that his friend's grandpa had done such a terrible thing to his grandpa, and couldn't help wondering whether Sooty was capable of tricking him just so *he* could win a competition.

His thoughts were disturbed by a loud crunching sound. It was coming from Beanie, who was hungry after the story and was munching noisily on her snacks. This in itself was not unusual. It was something else that made the young pup curious.

"Where did you get those from?" whispered Woody.

Beanie's cheeks were bulging and her mouth was too full to speak, so she lifted a paw and pointed to a group of rocks on the riverbank close to the den.

"LOOK!" yelled Woody, spying three small rafts and one big one that the Browns had last seen bobbing downstream in a cloud of angry bees. The rafts were now neatly anchored to the rocks on the riverbank. "Beanie has found all of our stuff!"

The Browns leapt up and hurried over to check that everything was still there, and then noticed another set of similar rafts that obviously belonged to the Black family.

"They must have found them and carried them upstream along with their own," said Mama Brown, heaving a sigh of relief. "That was awfully kind of them, don't you think?"

"Pirates!" growled Grandpa Bruno. "Those black-hearted black otters are not content with stealing our home, they want to sleep in our bedding and eat our food as well!"

"Oh, I'm sure that's not the case," said Papa Brown.

"Really?" said Grandpa. "Then where's the entrance to the den?"

The Browns all looked over at Cottonwood Lodge and squinted at the entrance – to find that, while they had been listening to a daring tale of rivalry and deception, the Blacks had swiftly fortified the tunnel entrance with a thick, sturdy door made of woven twigs!

Chapter Five

Reversal of Fortune

"That old swindler has done it this time!" said Grandpa Bruno, slipping into the water and untying the rafts. "Messing with me is one thing, but messing with my family is quite another! Now, everyone get in the water and start pushing these rafts towards the mooring pad, but don't let any of that lot see you."

The Browns followed Grandpa's instructions. They slowly edged the rafts across the river and drifted round to the side of the lodge. The Blacks, meanwhile, were all inside, peeping through the gaps in the door, wondering where their rivals had gone.

"I can't see them," said Mama Black, scanning the river. "They were there one minute and vanished the next."

"Those mysterious runaway rafts we found have drifted away from the bank," said Papa Black. "Though I think we know who they belong to now. Luckily, ours are still safe and secure."

"Never mind their rafts," said Grandpa Jack, squinting through the mesh of twigs. "You should be looking for that old crook, Bruno Brown. He's bound to be up to something slippery."

"What happened back when you were boxers, Grandpa?" asked Berry, the only girl among Sooty's five older siblings. The Black family knew all about their grandfather's glory days, but he never spoke of his old partner. "What was it that ended your friendship?"

"Never mind," said Grandpa Jack. "It's all in the past."

Jet, Coal, Storm and Shadow were all

keen that Grandpa Jack should tell the story too, but young Sooty didn't want to hear anything bad about his friend's grandfather.

"I feel awful for Woody and his family," said Sooty, hoping to change the subject. "The Browns are no different from us, really. And they have just lost their home."

The Blacks moved away from their makeshift door. Then Grandpa Jack, who seemed to be having second thoughts, said what everyone else was thinking.

"Bruno Brown may be a grizzled old rogue, but I wouldn't want to see any otters without a den," he said, patting Sooty's head. "So I hope your friend's family manage to turn their fortunes round and find somewhere to stay very soon."

"We have already, thanks," said Grandpa Bruno, standing in the central

 88

chamber with a ratty roll of bedding and an armful of food stores.

Behind him, the rest of the Browns all bundled in through the rear tunnel, laden with their stuff. Mama and Papa had swiftly unpacked the rafts on to the mooring pad and everyone had loaded up with whatever they could carry. Now both families were back inside the den, but only one of them had their belongings with them.

"I knew you'd be up to something sneaky," growled Jack.

"Well, you'd know all about that, wouldn't you?" said Bruno, pointing to the twiggy fortification over the entrance.

"Don't let the door bash your bottom on your way out!"

"We're not going anywhere!" growled Jack.

"You'll have to get your stuff sooner or later," said Bruno, and he hurried off with his family to fill the chambers with their things and claim them for the Browns.

The rest of the day saw the Black family running relays between the riverbank and the mooring pad, hopping over the stepping stones with their own supplies and bedding.

Then, while the Browns were occupied with dismantling the entrance door, the Blacks set about removing the Browns' belongings from half of the chambers and bringing in their own.

By the evening, both the Blacks and the Browns had moved in and taken four of the eight chambers each. The two families were determined to stay put and try to force the other out. The youngsters dug holes in the other pups' sleeping chambers, causing little leaks and soggy moss, and chanted rhymes about babies and bed-wetting.

There were also midnight plans of action, where a family's belongings – and sometimes its deep-sleeping members – were carried out of the den, placed on rafts and marooned on the riverbank. And for a whole week afterwards, everyone went about during the day being as loud and annoying as possible, which led to lots of snorts and squabbles and many squeals of otter frustration.

The only opposing otters that remained civil to each other were Mama Brown and Mama Black, who sat back and rolled their eyes at their families' escalating antics, and young Woody and Sooty, who were sad to see their siblings and elders at war with each other.

"I'm sorry for the way my family are behaving," said Woody as Nutmeg and Chestnut crept past with a rotten eel and threw it into an enemy chamber. "I don't know what's got into them."

"My family are just as bad," said Sooty as Storm and Shadow shot out after the

twins, covered in eel slime and hurling mud balls. "I think everyone could be friends if they would only get to know each other."

"I can't see that happening any time soon," sighed Woody.

"Me neither," sighed Sooty. "Everyone's gone bonkers."

The bad feeling reached its peak when both families decided to wash their paws in the same place at the same time. The indoor pool had brown and black otters all round it and, after much jostling and elbow-shoving, all eighteen of them ended up in the water, splashing so hard that the tranquil surface turned into a frothing, foaming whirlpool!

"ENOUGH!" growled Grandpa Bruno, standing up amid a churning broth of white water and otters. "We cannot live together under one roof, so one family must leave!"

"Excellent idea," said Grandpa Jack. "Off you go then."

"Actually, I propose a tournament!"

said Grandpa Bruno, ignoring his rival's comment as he threw down the challenge. "It's the only fair way to decide who should get to stay and who will have to leave."

Everyone stopped splashing and looked up at the two elderly otters, curious about what was being proposed. Did the grizzled old-timers really plan to turn the clock back to the night of the super heavyweight finals, all those years ago? And if it was a boxing tournament, did that mean they would all have to slug it out in the ring?

"I'll have no fighting!" warned Grandma Maple at the sight of Grandpa Bruno and Grandpa Jack glaring at each other like rival boxers at a weigh-in, eyes narrowed and whiskers bristling as they tried to stare each other out. "You'll have to think of something else you're both good at – apart from being stubborn, that is."

"We should all be able to get involved," said Grandpa Bruno, scratching his chin. "We have equal numbers, but different ages and abilities, so it should be something where everyone is well matched."

"Me and Sooty like making underwater obstacle courses," Woody said eagerly, grinning at his friend. "We're both really well matched at that."

"Good," said Grandpa Bruno. "Anyone else?"

"Us two are brilliant at volleyball!" said

96

Storm, high-fiving Shadow as they glanced around for a pair of likely challengers from the Brown family. "If any of you think you can take us on, that is."

"Bring it on!" said the twins, Chestnut and Nutmeg, teaming up for the first time ever.

"That's the spirit," said Grandpa Bruno, grinning broadly. "We'll have our very own river races to decide who gets to stay in Cottonwood Lodge, and everyone can compete in a different event."

"There's a mudslide out back," chirped Jet, jumping up, landing on the edge of the pool and assuming a surfing pose. The young otter had his fur stuck up in a Mohawk style with beeswax and considered himself

pretty cool. "I've been getting good at that over the last week if anyone wants to challenge me?"

"Ooooh, I'll take you up on that!" said Grandma Maple, clapping her paws together excitedly. "I was quite partial to a nice mudslide in my heyday."

"Huh?" said Jet, who didn't know what a heyday was, but had been expecting someone younger and a lot less female. "I have to compete with an old granny?"

"Unless you're chicken?" said Grandma Maple, pursing her lips and flapping her paws at her sides like wings. "Cluck-cluck, cluck-cluck!" she mocked, bobbing up and down.

"I'm no chicken!" squeaked Jet.

"Then that's decided," smiled Grandpa Bruno. "And I'm sure there will be events that we can all pair up and compete in. Everyone's good at something."

"Beanie's not good at anything," scoffed Coco.

"Except eating," added Nutmeg.

"And having an enormous tail," chuckled Chestnut.

"Leave her alone," said Woody. "Beanie's good at lots of things."

"I can hold my breath for quite a long time," Beanie whispered, and then disappeared under the water to prove it. Everyone waited patiently until she reappeared four minutes later, looking very pleased with herself.

"I can do that!" said Coal, waving at Beanie from across the pool.

"These party games all sound very jolly," growled Grandpa Jack, folding his arms and snorting through his nostrils, "but what about proper athletes like me? What am I supposed to do if I can't punch anything?"

"I didn't say you can't punch any*thing*,"

said Grandma Maple. "I would just prefer it if you didn't punch any*one*, like my husband. How do you feel about clamshells?"

"I like what's inside them," said Jack.

"Bruno cracks all my clamshells. I've never seen anyone stronger or faster," boasted Grandma Maple. "But if you're not up to the challenge, then I'm sure we'll understand…"

"I'll crack clamshells if that's what it takes to get you lot out of my den," Jack agreed reluctantly, and then frowned at his soggy family. "But I think the real challenge will be turning this jelly-bellied bunch into a lean, mean, fighting machine."

"I would have thought the *real* challenge

101

for you would be getting through the whole thing without cheating," mumbled Grandpa Bruno.

"What was that?" growled Grandpa Jack.

"Nothing," trilled Grandma Maple, shooing Grandpa Bruno and the rest of the Browns back to their chambers. All except Mama Brown, who refused to be shooed anywhere and hung back to have a word in private with Mama Black.

"We're not getting mixed up in all of this, are we?" she asked hopefully. Mama Brown had grown quite close to her dark-furred companion after a week of fishing and preparing food together. "It all seems a bit silly to me."

"Oh, I'm so glad you said that, my dear," sighed Mama Black, fanning herself with obvious relief. "River races indeed! What a load of old nonsense!"

And the pair scurried off together while Team Brown and Team Black grouped at opposite ends of the lodge to plan a strict regime for the beginning of training.

Chapter Six

Training Day

For Team Black, training meant the whole family rising at dawn and standing to attention in a neat line along the riverbank so Grandpa Jack could yell at them, jogging on the spot like a scary drill sergeant.

"I've never seen such a miserable bunch of water mammals in all my life!" he bellowed, moving down the line, prodding podgy bellies with a bulrush. "Winning this tournament is a matter of honour and family pride, so I will transform you fuzzy-furred blobs into lean, mean athletes, if it's the last thing I do. Now drop and give me twenty!"

The Black family stayed standing and looked at each other in bewilderment. They were unfamiliar with training jargon and had no idea what the grumpy old otter expected them to give him twenty of.

"Press-ups!" he yelled, rolling his eyes. "Twenty press-ups!"

The Blacks obediently dropped to the ground and began a series of swift, shallow press-ups, being short of arm and long in body as otters are. Everyone except the youngest pup, who remained on his hind legs, waving to his friend on the other side of the river.

"SOOTY BLACK!" bellowed Grandpa Jack, jogging over to his grandson, wiggling the bulrush irritably. "Are you with us or would you like to go and join the other team?"

"YES, PLEASE!" said Sooty, who would have liked nothing more than to train with Woody. Then he realised it wasn't really an option and quickly changed his answer.

"I mean, NO, SIR!" he yelled, and waved goodbye to his friend before launching into his press-ups.

Woody Brown stopped waving when his friend dropped out of sight, and turned back to the Brown family coaching session, led by Grandpa Bruno, whose approach to training was rather more laid-back.

"Should we wake him up?" whispered Beanie.

"I don't know," said Woody, frowning at Grandpa Bruno, who was snoring in a duet with Grandma Maple, both holding hands and drifting in circles in the water near the bank. Then he looked at the other members of Team Brown and sighed wearily. "Maybe we should just start packing."

Nutmeg and Chestnut were rolling around the riverbank, fighting over a clam, while Papa chased after them, trying to split them up *and* nab the clam for himself. Coco was grooming her fur with her back to everyone, refusing to join in because training sounded very unglamorous and, even worse, wet. Though she still found time to tease Beanie, telling her younger sister that she probably shouldn't take part because there was no way she could win.

Mama Brown had got up before everyone else and was nowhere to be seen. This was also true of Mama Black, which at least kept the competition even.

Woody didn't want to train either, especially as he would have to compete against his best friend, Sooty. But he didn't want his family to lose their home, so he tiptoed to the water's edge and prodded Grandpa Bruno with a stick.

The old otter snuffled awake and quickly nudged his wife.

"Where was I?" he frowned, scuttling out of the water and on to a rock. He remembered waking everyone up at sunrise and asking them to join him on the riverbank, but the rest was a bit of a blur.

"You said we all looked tired and needed a pep talk," said Woody.

"But then you fell asleep and slid into

the river," said Beanie.

"So Grandma went in after you to wake you up," added Woody, scratching his head as he relayed the events of the last few minutes. "But then she fell asleep too."

"What are they saying?" asked Grandma Maple, lifting her hearing-shell up to her ear. "Something about poo?"

"Not poo," said Grandpa Bruno. "*Too!*"

"Two what?" asked Grandma Maple.

The general confusion was interrupted by shouting on the other side of the river where the Black family were being chased up and down the bank with a floppy bulrush. Grandpa Jack was barking insults at them as they ran in a military formation.

"YOU BIG, LAZY LUMPS!"

"GET THOSE FAT KNEES UP!"

"COME ON, WOBBLE-BOTTOM!"

Grandpa Bruno looked back at his ragtag

team, made up of squabbling twins, sulking

teens and young pups looking utterly lost, and knew he needed to raise their spirits with a few wise words.

"*Two* families!" Grandpa Bruno boomed loudly, pulling his shoulders back and standing proud upon the rock. He gestured with one paw to the Blacks, who were now doing synchronised star jumps, and with the other paw to his own untidy brood. "Two families and only one den, so we have a mighty challenge ahead of us!"

The twins stopped fighting for a moment and came closer. Woody held Beanie's paw and Papa Brown stood behind them. Even Coco shuffled round to hear what Grandpa had to say.

The old otter suddenly felt the pressure of younger eyes upon him and cast his mind back to his boxing days for the things that had inspired him then and turned him into a champion…

"Get those fat knees up, you big, lazy lump!" laughed young Jack Black, jogging with his best friend Bruno Brown down the hazy riverbank. The black otter broke away and sprinted ahead, coaxing his companion to catch up with him. "Come on, wobble-bottom!"

Young Bruno could barely run for laughing, but his friend's encouragement made him dig deep for that extra burst of energy, like he always did when they trained together.

The otters were neck and neck as they made it to the arena for their usual sparring practice – and then promptly collapsed into a heap.

It was the morning before the tournament and they were both very excited. But despite his outward confidence, Jack Black didn't always have belief in himself.

"I hope I pass the first round," said Jack.

"You will," said Bruno. "We're in the best shape of our careers!"

"But what if I don't get through?" asked Jack.

"All you can do is try your best," said Bruno, whose style of encouragement was calmer and more thoughtful than his friend's colourful banter. "And know that I'll be cheering you on, whatever happens."

"You too, my friend," said Jack.

"Friends forever!" they cheered.

Grandpa Bruno felt a paw slip into his and Grandma Maple appeared beside him. He suddenly realised that it was his friend who had inspired him and made him a champion. Jack Black and Bruno Brown had supported each other. But now he had a family and they were looking to him for guidance and support.

"Two families!" he repeated.

"You already said that, you forgetful old goat!" roared a voice from the other side of the river. "Are you encouraging your team or trying to bore them to death?"

"Mind your own business!" growled Bruno, shaking his fist.

Jack blew a raspberry in response and then barked at his team to give him ten squat-thrusts on the double, which they quickly did. Grandpa Jack was secretly pleased with his family, but he kept one eye on his old rival all the same.

Grandpa Bruno saw that he was being spied upon, hopped down from the rock and huddled with his family. "There's only one thing you need to do to win," he whispered gruffly. "And that's to try your best."

"And then we'll definitely win?" asked Woody.

"Not necessarily," said Grandpa, tapping

his nose. "But if you've tried your best and played a fair game then, win or lose, you will be able to hold your head up high."

"And that's particularly true if you no longer have a roof over it," said Grandma Maple, popping her husband's romantic bubble. "And we won't have a roof over our heads if we don't win."

"Another good point!" said Bruno, narrowing his eyes. "So to make *sure* you try your best, I'll probably have to bark some pretty unflattering insults at you."

"HOORAY!" cheered the Browns, who thought Team Black's training looked like enormous fun. So they all put their paws together and pledged to try their best and not take Grandpa's yelling to heart, and they cheered before breaking away.

Team Brown swiftly gathered in a line – far less tidy than Team Black's – and began their training. They now felt very cheerful and were having a brilliant time, with Grandpa shouting about how fat and useless they were, which proved to be all the encouragement they needed.

Each team stayed on their side of the river as the two old boxers, who obviously had a score to settle, put them through their paces. The otters ran and jumped and swam and by the evening Team Brown and Team Black were fighting fit and seemed very evenly matched. They

had been so focused on the training and
making practical preparations for the river
races, that no one noticed they were being

watched from two high rocks above.

"Who do you think will win, my dear?" Mama Brown called over to Mama Black on the other side of the river. The pair had been sunbathing all day, tossing clams and mussels to each other and swapping family stories.

"I wouldn't like to say," said Mama Black, looking back and forth between the banks, comparing the two families. "But I think, as far as teams go, you and I are definitely in the lead."

"Oh, I quite agree," said Mama Brown. She squinted at the sunset and realised it was almost dinner time. "Shall we go inside and prepare some food for the troops?"

"Good idea," replied Mama Black as she brushed broken mussel shells off her rock and into the water. "And I think they will need an extra large feast ahead of their big day tomorrow!"

Chapter Seven

The River Races

The day of the river races was bright and sunny and everyone was in high spirits. Team Brown was warming up on the mooring pad, doing star jumps and squat-thrusts, when Team Black jogged out of the den and gathered alongside them. The otters all appeared focused on preparing for their challenges, but each one was secretly flicking sideways glances, sizing up the competition.

At the start, Grandma Maple, who would act as referee for all events except her own, clambered on to a specially constructed diving platform and addressed the assembled otters.

"Welcome to the first and only river races!" she said, holding up her paws in a wide, welcoming gesture as the two families cheered, whooped and clapped in excitement. "A day of sports and games, yes. But also a competition to decide who wins the right to live in Cottonwood Lodge and who will have to leave."

The families cheered and whistled again, each confident that their own team would win the right to stay while the other would be packing up their rafts again.

"I wish you all the best of luck," said Maple, looking out across a sea of brown and black furry faces, bright eyes gazing up at her. "And most importantly, everyone should have fun!"

Mama Black and Mama Brown watched from the bank with intrigue and disapproval in equal measure. They were preparing food and refreshments for the teams, but otherwise refused to take part in any way. And although each of them wanted her own family to win, neither wished the other family to leave.

"The first event will be the triathlon," said Grandma Maple, stepping aside to make room for Papa Black and Papa Brown, who joined her on the platform. "A high-dive, speed-swim and overland-sprint spectacular!"

"WOO HOO!" cheered the teams, the young pups jumping up and down as their fathers mounted the diving boards, bobbing and stretching in a businesslike manner before nodding to the referee.

"LET THE GAMES BEGIN!" yelled Grandma Maple, lifting up her horn-shaped hearing-shell, puffing out her cheeks and

blowing into it as hard as she could.

HOOOOOOONK!

Papa Black and Papa Brown bounced on their diving boards, somersaulted in mid-air and plunged into the river, both dives so skilful that little separated them in the first section of the triathlon. Once in the water,

they swam as fast as they could against the
current, glistening bodies soaring in and
out of the river as their families gathered

along the bank and cheered them on.

"COME ON, SON!" yelled Grandpa Jack.

"YEAH, COME ON, SON!" yelled Grandpa Bruno, not to be outdone.

The speed-swim section ended upon reaching and circling a group of rocks far upstream. There, the two otters leapt out of the water and began the third and final overland-sprint section. They landed on the bank together and hit the ground running as they doubled back to the finishing line.

"I must say I'm impressed," panted Papa Brown, sprinting as fast as he could towards the cheering crowd. "I could do with an otter as fast as you as my fishing partner!"

"That's very kind of you to say so," panted Papa Black, imagining for a moment all the fish two strong swimmers could catch by working together. "I was thinking exactly the same thing!"

It was neck and neck until the end, but Papa Brown lost by a whisker to Papa Black and they both collapsed in a wet furry heap. The panting husbands had landed at the feet of their wives who, instead of praising their efforts, just glanced up briefly from the preparation of riverweed wraps and rolled their eyes.

For the next event, Grandma Maple went head-to-head with Jet Black down the longest, loopiest, muckiest mudslide any of them had ever seen. It sloped from the towering treeline beyond the riverbank, twisted and turned through two bumpy verges and then briefly levelled out before plunging down a steep slide, ending with a final ramp at the water's edge.

"I'm not sure about this, Maple Moo," whispered Grandpa Bruno, gazing up at the slippery, slopey slide. "It looks too dangerous. You might do yourself a mischief!"

"I've slid down bigger slides than that with my eyes shut," scoffed Grandma Maple, cuddling Grandpa Bruno before heading up the hill. "But thank you for worrying. Now you know how I felt watching you go off boxing every evening."

"May I help you to the top, Mrs Brown?" asked Jet, holding out a paw to the old otter. The young otter's Mohawk had extra beeswax to withstand the G-force.

"You may indeed, young pup," said Grandma Maple, gripping the black otter's arm with both paws. "It's nice to see a young otter with good manners who looks out for his elders, but don't think this means I'll go easy on you when we reach the top."

"No, ma'am," said Jet as they carefully climbed the steep, slippery bank.

Mama Brown and Mama Black also held each other's paws as they watched their elderly mother and young son teeter to the top of the giant mudslide and, when the horn sounded, they held their breath as the fearless otters leapt off the ledge.

"WOO HOO!" yelled Grandma Maple, landing on her hind paws and surfing the mudflow. She used her tail as a rudder to steer and stay upright as the wind blasted through her fur.

"WHOOOAAAAH!" yelled Jet, who landed on his bottom and spun like a sycamore seed. He had been down many fewer mudslides than his ancient rival, but he made up for it by being more flexible, and levelled out in no time, rolling on to his belly to shoot under her legs like a rocket.

"Oh, no, you don't, young whippersnapper!" laughed Maple, zigzagging behind him so she could work up extra speed. The old otter sprang off her tail and leapt over Jet, paws landing in the mud just before the curve of the take-off ramp, which she hit at speed and shot back in the air again.

"WHEEEEEEEEE!" squealed Maple, doing a loop-the-loop, and then she plunged into the water, emerging victorious just as Jet Black soared over her head and did a massive bellyflop behind her.

"Go, Grandma!" cheered Woody Brown, jumping up and down and whooping at the top of his voice. The old otter's triumph was so spectacular that his friend joined in too.

133

"Go, Mrs Brown!" cheered Sooty Black, whooping and jumping up and down with his friend, until he caught sight of his frowning family and remembered whose side he was on!

The two friends had been having so much fun together, sharing snacks and following the river races, that they kept forgetting they were on rival teams.

Next up was the special water-volleyball match between Nutmeg and Chestnut Brown, and Storm and Shadow Black. An old fishing net found at the bottom of the river was stretched between the two banks just above the waterline. Then a clamshell was flipped to decide who would go first, and the twins, who called it correctly, were handed a tightly bound twig-ball.

"Come on, Browns!" yelled the Browns, gathered on one side of the river, while the Blacks cheered and whooped for their team from the opposite bank.

Nutmeg tossed the ball high in the air, spun in the water and whacked it with her tail as she rolled, head emerging again as her tail vanished, just in time to see the twig-ball soar over the net.

The ball headed for Shadow who, instead of hitting it with his paws, rolled in the water too and batted it back with his tail for a high-speed volley that shot over the net and headed straight for Chestnut. The

young otter had never seen anything move so fast, especially not coming towards his head. He dived immediately, not so he could hit the ball, but to escape it!

The first point went to Storm and Shadow, who cheered and high-fived each other. But there was no such team spirit on the Browns' side of the net.

"You should have hit that!" yelled Nutmeg, splashing her brother.

"If I hadn't dodged, that ball would have knocked my head off!" protested Chestnut.

"It might have knocked some sense into you!" Nutmeg mocked.

"Let's see how much better you do when it's zooming in your direction!" said

Chestnut, folding his arms in a huff.

The game resumed and this time it was Nutmeg dodging as Storm served a sideswipe, the twiggy ball spinning and whistling angrily as it whizzed through the air.

"Eeeek!" squealed Nutmeg, ducking underwater. When she emerged, the young otter saw more triumphant high-fiving on the other side of the net.

"See!" said Chestnut.

And then the Brown twins swam towards each other and did something they had never done before. They agreed to put every one of their squabbles aside and team up together, joining forces against their more formidable opponents.

The Browns began to play much better once they started working as a team. They hoisted each other up to hit high balls and tackled incoming spinners by batting together so they could handle the impact of the shots and volleys at double speed. They still lost out to Storm and Shadow, who were carried away on the shoulders of Team Black, but Nutmeg and Chestnut had had the best time ever.

"You were so quick on that last volley!" gasped Chestnut as they made their way back to Team Brown, who were cheering on the bank just as loudly as if they'd actually won.

"Thanks," said Nutmeg, ruffling her brother's fur. "And your last serve wasn't too bad either. For a boy, that is!"

"Oi!" squeaked Chestnut, and the twins were squabbling again in no time, chasing each other in circles as Team Brown and Team Black made their way upstream for the next event.

No one knew what it was going to be because Coco and Berry had created it between themselves. All anyone knew was that the older girls had gone off together after the triathlon, and had decided that they both wanted to join in the games, but definitely didn't want to get their heads wet.

Now both teams were invited to watch and judge their mysterious event, and even Mama Brown and Mama Black attended out of sheer curiosity.

"It's the least we can do," said Mama Brown.

"The very least," agreed Mama Black.

The two families gathered at a bay-like section of river, not far from the lodge, that was surrounded by large willow trees. The area had small, scattered islands of rocks and reeds that slowed the flow of water to a ripple, making it appear almost still. The audience sat and watched in hushed silence as Coco and Berry tiptoed out across an overhanging branch, with lilies adorning

their heads, and then eased themselves
into the river.

A light breeze was making the tendrils
of willow leaves hiss pleasantly as the
two young otters glided about in a
synchronised water-dance, their heads
and floral headdresses remaining firmly
above the waterline so they kept dry
the whole time.

The dance
looked graceful
and serene on
the surface,
but involved a
lot of ferocious
swimming below.

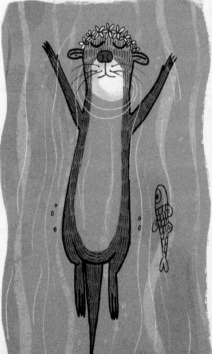

When it finished, the audience gave a standing ovation and marked their scores in the mud, which showed that Coco was the winner. Berry had no problem with losing to Coco. She knew that her swimming partner had been training her whole life in the art of keeping her head dry.

The next event offered less elegant entertainment than the lily dance, with the two grandpas going head-to-head in a rock-pounding clam-slam! And they were literally head to head, as Grandpa Bruno and Grandpa Jack were both floating on the water, their heads pressed together so neither could see how many clams the other had cracked until the horn-honk signalled the end. This was a rapid game of speed and accuracy, and no one would know who had won until the official clam-count.

"On your marks…" said Grandma Maple, with Woody and Sooty treading water beside their grandpas, each holding a floating basket full of clams. "Rocks at the ready…" she added as her husband and his rival positioned flat rocks on their bellies.

HOOOOOONK!

With the signal, Grandpa Bruno and Grandpa Jack each grabbed a clam from their basket, gripped it in two paws and began whacking it on the flat stone until the shell broke open.

CRACK!

CRACK!

They popped the clam meat in the baskets and tossed the shells back into the river. Everything was so fast and furious it needed a lot of concentration, but that didn't stop the old otters hurling insults along the way. *CRACK!*

"Have you done any yet?" asked Grandpa Bruno, throwing another clam into his basket. "No one will think any the worse of you if you're too old and feeble."

CRACK!

"Don't mistake that cracking noise for your rickety old joints," said Grandpa Jack, tossing more broken shells into the water. "It was the sound of another clam surrendering to my awesome paws!"

CRACK!

"More like snoresome paws!" scoffed Grandpa Bruno.

CRACK!

"And there goes another one!" mocked Jack.

"You probably weakened them all in advance," said Bruno, hammering away at a particularly stubborn clam. "I know you don't like to leave too much to chance."

CRACK!

"Me?" growled Jack. "You're a fine one to talk!"

And with this, Grandma Maple honked on the shell-horn and brought a swift end to the event before things got out of hand. The clams were counted and Grandpa Jack had cracked almost twice as many as Grandpa Bruno. The old enemies only snorted at each other and swam back to their families. Sooty and Woody were left behind, feeling bad.

They knew that their grandpas had been the very best of friends, just like them, but now they couldn't even bear being in the same section of river at the same time.

"I was hoping the river races would revive their friendship," sighed Woody. "That they would remember why they liked each other before and forget all about their silly feud."

"Me too," said Sooty. "But they really can't stand each other."

"I've never seen my grandpa so grumpy before," added Woody.

"Mine neither," said Sooty. "He keeps scowling."

"Don't worry, young pups," Grandma Maple consoled them as she helped the two little ones back to the bank with their baskets. "Those two were not always so crabby, and there may yet be hope for them."

It was time for what was probably the least exciting event, but it was the one Woody most wanted the Browns to win. And it had nothing to do with Cottonwood

Lodge. This was Beanie's event and he wanted her to show Coco and the twins how brilliant she was. He got to his sister just in time.

"... so if you lose, we'll all be homeless," Chestnut said to Beanie.

"We might as well start packing now!" added Nutmeg.

"Leave her alone," said Woody.

"But they're right," whispered Beanie. "If you add up the scores of the teams so far, the Blacks have won three events and we've only won two."

"But there's still Sooty's and my underwater obstacle race to come," said Woody, who had already counted and knew there were seven events in total. "It's not over yet."

"But if Beanie loses this one, it'll be four wins to two, so even if you win the last one, we'll still lose Cottonwood Lodge," said Coco, fiddling with her lily headdress. She liked it so much she had decided to keep it on.

"It's a shame she's not competing in a 'Huge Tail' event," said Chestnut. "She'd probably win that."

"Or eating," said Nutmeg. "She'd win at eating."

"I won my event," said Coco, just in case anyone had forgotten.

"It doesn't matter who wins," said Woody,

getting cross with his older siblings. "And it won't be Beanie's fault if we lose. We're competing as a family and we're all doing our best."

"But—" said the twins.

"Beanie was cheering more loudly than anyone during the volleyball," Woody interrupted. "And she carried on cheering even when you didn't win, because that's what families do!"

He braced himself, ready for the twins and his big sister to pounce on him, as they usually did when he argued with them, but this time they did something completely unexpected.

"Sorry, Beanie," said the twins, looking

genuinely apologetic.

"Yeah, I'm sorry too," added Coco, patting her little sister's head. "And we promise not to blame you when you don't win."

"Oh, shut up, stinky bottom!" said Woody, and he grabbed Beanie's paw and ran off towards the pool for her event, shouting over his shoulder, "Beanie is going to win!"

"Ooo, you little...!" shrieked Coco, chasing after him.

At the pool, Coal was already in the water, so Beanie jumped in too. Woody joined the other brown otters, keeping his distance from Coco, who had arrived with the twins just in time.

"This event is to see who can hold their breath underwater for the longest time," said Grandma Maple, standing on the edge of the pool as she introduced the two shy contestants. "Are you both ready to begin?"

Beanie and Coal nodded and smiled.

"Then the last one up is the winner!" said Maple, lifting her shell-horn.

HOOOOOONK!

Beanie and Coal breathed in deeply and slowly submerged, swimming down to the bottom of the pool where they sat, cheeks bulging, as they held their breath. Occasionally they waved at each other, but mostly they peered up towards the light, at the silhouettes of their families, who were all waving at them and cheering them on. Beanie felt proud seeing Coco and the twins rooting for her, but the loudest cheers came from Woody.

Four minutes in, she was still quite happy at the bottom of the pool, but Coal was looking uncomfortable, having to use quite a lot of energy and oxygen flapping his paws to stay submerged. Beanie managed this much more easily as her huge tail and heavier weight provided extra ballast. She was so happy that she stayed underwater for a whole minute more to enjoy her triumph after Coal gave up and swam to the surface, and when Beanie resurfaced she was greeted by riotous applause from her family.

The twins lifted Beanie up and gave her a victory lap on their shoulders, while Coco chased Woody around them, which didn't do Coco's lily headdress any good at all.

The excitement was high in both camps now the Browns and the Blacks had three wins each, and there was only one event to go – the underwater obstacle race with Woody and Sooty!

Chapter Eight

An Unexpected Obstacle

Everyone was excited about the underwater obstacle race between Woody and Sooty, but they were all hungry too. Luckily, Mama Black and Mama Brown had laid out a huge fishy buffet for the athletes, so the teams agreed to resume the racing after lunch.

The day had begun with a definite divide between the two families, but after watching and competing in the exciting events, they were now mingling and chatting cheerfully. The young otters had had great fun spending time together, and even Papa Black and Papa Brown found they had a lot in common, just like their wives. Woody and Sooty enjoyed the sight of their families getting along so well, as it meant they could laugh and play without feeling guilty about letting their teams down. All was going swimmingly until Grandpa Bruno and Grandpa Jack reached for the same fish.

"Oh, no, you don't!" growled Jack, tugging on the slippery fish tail.

"Nice try!" growled Bruno, tugging on the slippery fish head.

"Let go, you crooked old toad!"

"You let go, you sly old crow!"

"I saw it first!"

"Well, I grabbed it first!"

"Stop!" yelled Grandma Maple, but it was already too late.

The fish shot up in the air and everyone craned their necks skywards, watching as it landed in the river with a loud *PLOP!* And when they looked back, the two old otters were rolling around the bank in a furious ball of brown and black fur.

Team Black and Team Brown quickly re-formed and pulled their senior members apart, arms and legs swiping at the air like a pair of upturned turtles.

"I've had just about enough of you and your jibes!" growled Grandpa Jack, rising up and dusting himself off. "Let's get on with the last event and out of each other's lives forever!"

"I'll second that," said Grandpa Bruno, flicking mud off his fur. "Let's put an end to this so we don't have to spend any more time together!"

With help from Papa Brown and Papa Black, Woody and Sooty had spent a good portion of the previous day building a large obstacle course for their event in the competition. The course had hoops and tunnels, ladders and funnels, all going in and out of the water, followed by a final short dash to the finish line.

Before mounting their diving boards at the start of the course, the two friends hugged and wished each other the best of luck. The pair looked down at their families, who were waving and cheering, all except for the grandpas, who had their arms folded and were scowling at each other.

"Do you promise to stay friends?" asked Woody, who was worried about competing against his friend – because for one to win, the other would have to lose. "No matter who wins the obstacle course and gets to stay in the den?"

"I promise," said Sooty.

"Me too," said Woody.

"But what if one of us gets cross because they lost the race?" asked Sooty. "Our grandpas probably thought they'd always be friends, and now they can't stand one another."

Woody thought about it for a moment and wondered how he would feel if he lost out to his friend. Then he smiled broadly. "We won't be like that," he said confidently.

"How can you be so sure?" asked Sooty.

"Because we will be on each other's side as well as on our own," said Woody. "I want to win the race myself because I don't want my family to have to move to another den, but I'll still be happy for you if you win, because you're my best friend."

"I'll be happy if you win too," said Sooty.

"I think our grandpas must have forgotten what's important, and that's why they don't like each other any more," said Woody, holding out a paw. "So let's make a pact always to be on each other's side, and that way we'll never cheat and always win and stay best friends forever."

Sooty and Woody shook paws to seal the pact and were both beaming. They could now enjoy the competition just like they enjoyed racing together for fun because, whatever else was at stake, they knew their friendship was safe.

"Are you ready, my darlings?" asked Grandma Maple, clambering up on to the platform. The two pups shuffled on to the diving boards, took a few practice bounces and nodded. "Then may the best otter win!" she said, lifting the shell-horn to her puffed-out cheeks.

"May the best otter win!" echoed Woody and Sooty.

HOOOOOONK!

The sound of the horn gave way to a huge cheer as Woody and Sooty bounced, backflipped and plunged into the river for the final race.

Underwater, the cheering was muffled as the two friends swam deep, bodies wiggling in waves, their hind paws flattened like tail fins to generate speed. They reached the twiggy tunnels along the bottom of the river and darted through, their tails steering like submarine rudders. On the other side of the tunnels the otters shot straight up, burst out of the water and soared through the first of a series of hoops. Woody and Sooty were neck and neck after the first obstacle and were really enjoying themselves, their families running along the riverbank cheering them on.

The next challenge was to weave through a ladder that was anchored to the riverbed with rocks and stretched all the way up to the surface where the top was tied to a large floating raft. The friends dived down to the bottom again and snaked through the ladder rungs, overtaking each other several times before they reached the top. There, they scampered over the raft towards

another waiting hoop.

"HOORAY!" cheered the Brown family as Woody went through first, which put him in the lead.

"Come on, Sooty!" cheered the Black family, encouraging their youngest member as he followed through the hoop.

Next, Woody and Sooty had to scale rocks, dive through rings, climb ropes and slide down tubes. Hoop jumps marked the end of each obstacle and the beginning of the next, and Woody managed to hold his lead, jumping through each hoop just before Sooty.

The last obstacle was an underwater speed swim through a swaying forest of dense riverweed. Even with his head start, Woody Brown swam faster than ever before, shooting through the tangle of weeds like a furry torpedo! As he reached the end he could see the final stretch and the blurry silhouettes of the families at the finish line. They were all jumping up and down with excitement as they waited for the otter pups to emerge.

I'm going to win! thought Woody, the added thrill of victory spurring him on. *I'm going to win for my family and we will all get to stay in Cottonwood Lodge!*

But then he remembered that his win

would mean a loss for his friend. And not only that, but the Black family would have to clear out and move away.

Woody glanced back to see how close his friend was to catching him up and whether there could possibly be a tie, only to discover that Sooty was nowhere to be seen!

The young pup couldn't have fallen that far behind!

Woody didn't hesitate for a second. He immediately doubled back and re-entered the forest of riverweed, darting back and forth amid the swirling tendrils, searching for his friend. Shoals of silver fish dashed away and tiny bubbles plumed around him, and then he saw a small black paw waving at him in the distance.

It occurred to Woody that Sooty could be tricking him, luring him back just so he could overtake and sprint for the finish line. That's probably what Grandpa Bruno would think if he was racing Grandpa Jack, but Woody knew his friend wouldn't do such a thing.

They had made a pact, after all.

Woody dashed through the weeds and reached Sooty just in time. His friend was waving all four paws frantically but seemed rooted to the spot. Woody ripped the weeds away to discover that Sooty's tail was tangled in a scrap of fishing net wrapped round a large rock. From the panicked look on Sooty's face, Woody could tell the struggle had used up most of his air. The obstacle race no longer mattered. It was now a race against time!

Woody tugged at the fishing net, trying to break it with his paws or tear it with his teeth, but it was too strong and only tightened its grip on Sooty's tail. The young rescuer darted away and searched the riverbed until he found a half-shell, then he used the sharp edge to hack through the netting and eventually managed to free his friend.

Sooty needed to get to the surface quickly, so he sped away, rushing upwards through the water until he broke the surface and gasped for air. From the murky depths, Woody watched with relief as his friend struggled to the finish line and was lifted out of the river.

Relaxing now that Sooty was safe, Woody made his way to the surface too, but instead of worried faces when he reached the finish line, he saw the Black family rejoicing with the young pup up on their shoulders, celebrating his amazing triumph. Not only had Sooty won the final event, he had also put the Blacks in the lead, making them the rightful owners of

Cottonwood Lodge.

Woody looked over at his own family, who appeared deflated.

"Never mind," said Mama and Papa Brown as he swam towards them and climbed out of the water. "We know you did your best. We all did, but the Blacks were just better and won the competition fair and square."

"I guess so," said Woody, watching the winning family singing and cheering, hurrying back along the bank towards the den. He could see Sooty bobbing up and down as they carried him with them, but his friend didn't even look back.

Chapter Nine

Otter Chaos!

The Black family was still celebrating, splashing around in the river and cheering when the Brown family arrived back at Cottonwood Lodge. The Browns knew they had to move out before they outstayed their welcome, so they went inside to pack their things.

One by one, the Blacks followed them in to say their goodbyes.

Berry gave Coco her floral headdress to remember her by. Shadow and Storm presented Chestnut and Nutmeg with the twiggy volleyball. Jet gave Grandma Maple some Mohawk beeswax, which she fully intended to use. Coal didn't know what to say to Beanie, being even more shy than her, but Beanie was feeling braver after her win so she gave him a huge hug that almost took his breath away. Papa Black told Papa Brown about a small den upstream that was vacant, and Mama Black packed a large food hamper for the journey and handed it to Mama Brown, both dabbing tears from their eyes.

Grandpa Jack didn't come to wish a fond farewell to Grandpa Bruno, but that didn't surprise anyone after their history and the recent fight. The big surprise was that little Sooty Black didn't come to see Woody Brown.

"Maybe he's too upset," said Mama Brown as the family gathered in the central chamber with all of their belongings. "Imagine how you would feel if you won the race and your friend had to leave."

Woody wasn't sure what to think after what had happened during the obstacle race, but Sooty was his best friend and, in the spirit of their pact, he decided to trust him. They had promised to be on each other's side, after all. Which meant that if Sooty didn't come to say goodbye, then he probably had a very good reason.

Farewells were exchanged and a few more tears were shed as the Browns loaded up their rafts on the mooring pad and tethered them all together, this time with double knots. The Blacks looked at the huge, empty lodge and suddenly felt that maybe it was too big for just one family.

The Browns were about to enter the water when a young voice stopped them in their tracks.

"WAIT!" yelled Sooty Black, running

 out of the den. He was holding Grandpa Jack's paw, tugging the old otter along behind him. "My grandpa wants to ask you all something!"

"This should be good," growled Grandpa Bruno drily.

"My grandson has just told me what happened in the last race," gasped Grandpa Jack, catching his breath. "That young Woody rescued him from the riverweeds and probably saved his life, and that if he hadn't gone back for his friend, then he would have won."

The Browns gasped and looked at Woody.

"Is this true?" asked Mama and Papa Brown. Woody nodded awkwardly.

"So I want to ask if you would consider staying here in Cottonwood Lodge with us," said Grandpa Jack, opening his arms in a welcoming gesture. "We all seem to get on quite well together – most of us, anyway," he added, scowling at Grandpa Bruno, but then he smiled at him and offered to shake his paw. "But I'm prepared to put our silly feud to rest, if you are, old friend."

Grandpa Bruno looked at the paw-shaped peace offering through narrowed eyes.

Then he frowned and scratched his whiskers as he considered the offer and took a step forward.

"Old friend?" he said.

Grandpa Jack nodded and smiled awkwardly.

"Nice try, you old swindler, but I'm on to you this time!" growled Grandpa Bruno. "If my grandson threw the race to save your grandson, then I think Cottonwood Lodge should be ours! And then *we* will decide who else might get to stay!"

The two old otters began to snort through their nostrils as the old feud came flooding back. It was as though the boxing match that broke their friendship had happened yesterday and they both still felt bitterly betrayed.

So, after the brief excitement at Woody Brown's bravery and Grandpa Jack's offer, it became very clear to both families that their grandpas could never forgive each other. And that meant the Browns and the Blacks could never live together...

"Enough!" yelled Grandma Maple, stepping forward. "After all these years, I can't keep the secret to myself any longer. Neither of you stubborn old goats cheated the other!"

"HUH?" gasped Jack and Bruno.

"It was me!" sighed Grandma Maple, sitting down heavily on a rock. She was so

relieved to have her terrible secret out in the open that she was now very anxious to set the record straight. "It was the night of the final fight, and young Bruising Bruno and Big Bad Jack had grown further apart with every match…"

"Promise me you'll be all right," said Maple, pacing up and down nervously while Bruno skipped and cross-skipped with a length of rope. "I don't know what I'd do if anything happened to you…"

"I'll be fine," Bruno said confidently. "I know Jack's moves better than he knows them himself. By the end of the night I'll be the first ever five-time super heavyweight champion."

"Then what?" sighed Maple, sitting on a log to rest her legs. They had been aching lately so she rubbed them with fish oil to soothe her weary muscles. She had not told Bruno that they were expecting a litter of pups in the spring, which caused her to feel tired and more worried about him than usual.

"I'll be fine," said Bruno again, trying to reassure Maple by holding her paws in his gloves. "And when I win this tournament, the Otter Boxing Federation will take me on a grand boxing tour up and down the river, and you can come with me. We'll be living the high life, Maple Moo!"

But Maple had no interest in living the high life. She wanted nothing more than to settle down and raise a family with her beloved Bruno. She also worried that, if he won the match that evening, he would want to continue boxing and might get injured or worse...

Maple couldn't bear the thought of anything happening to the otter she loved. So when she lifted Bruno's gloves and noticed how they glistened in the moonlight with her slippery fish oil, Maple remained silent, knowing full well that he would lose the match to Big Bad Jack.

"So it was me who rubbed fish oil into your gloves, not Jack," Maple finished her story, mopping tears from her eyes. "It was me who put an end to your boxing career for my own selfish reasons."

184

Everyone looked from her to Grandpa Bruno, who struggled to piece everything together and didn't know how to react to Grandma Maple's shocking revelation. Then he took his wife's paws within his own, as he had done all those years ago, and hugged her tightly.

"I would never have fought that night if I'd known, Maple Moo," said Grandpa Bruno. "And I would have chosen raising a family together over a silly boxing tour any day of the week. Just look at our wonderful family!"

"Really?" gasped Maple. "You don't have any regrets?"

"My only regret is that I didn't trust my

best friend," said Bruno.

"I planned to tell you," sobbed Maple. "But then the pups came and we didn't see Jack on the river again – not until we arrived here, and by then I didn't know how to tell you that he'd done nothing wrong."

"I shouldn't have needed to be told," said Bruno. "I should have known myself that Jack wouldn't cheat, and I should have trusted him always to be on my side, even when we were competing against each other."

Woody and Sooty exchanged a knowing smile, and everyone looked from Grandpa Bruno to Grandpa Jack, who quickly wiped his eyes and sniffed gruffly. The old black otter had also thought his friend had cheated by offering an oily glove to shake, so he was just as guilty of mistrust.

"We've both been stubborn and foolish and wasted so many years because of our silly pride," said Grandpa Jack, offering his paw once more. "Can we be friends again?"

Bruno ignored the paw and gave his best friend a huge hug, and everyone else was so moved that they all joined in. Papa Black hugged Papa Brown, Berry hugged Coco, Chestnut hugged Shadow, Storm hugged Nutmeg, Beanie hugged Coal, Grandma Maple hugged Jet, and Woody hugged Sooty. Mama Black and Mama Brown looked at everyone else hugging, rolled their eyes, and then they hugged too. It was like a final 'Hugging' event in the competition, where everyone was a winner!

"HOORAY!" cheered the Browns.

And because it sounded like fun, the Blacks tried it too.

"HOORAY!" cheered the Blacks.

And then, since the two families were about to start living together and sharing everything, they decided that the best way to begin their new life was by sharing a cheer all together.

"HOORAY!"

Epilogue

So the Brown family moved back into Cottonwood Lodge with the Black family and lived happily ever after. No one had a room to themselves, so there were farts and snores at bedtime. The mamas and papas became rather competitive, and

Grandpa Jack and Grandpa Bruno found brand-new things to fall out about, much to the annoyance of Grandma Maple. Even Woody and Sooty learnt to disagree, as best friends often do, but on one thing everyone was agreed. Living together was otter chaos, and that was exactly how they liked it!